LEAVES OF SAND

Patrick Nickles

CONTENTS

Prologue

The Subway

Where can we find reality? Where are the real faces, the sincere smiles and understanding eyes, the authentic and outstretched hands?

Everyday, millions scurried in and out of the subways, buses, trams, and trains, with faces obscured with cloth, on their way to enclosed offices and workspaces. For most of them, work was a series of electronic exchanges and virtual meetings with no real interaction or meaning. People barely met in person. So for most, attire became daily uniforms, etiquette, became irrelevant anachronisms in a conceptual universe where the only real thing was the badge.

The badge. This alternate reality contained every single piece of information known about any individual who succumbed to its spell, their families, their family photos, their addresses, languages, education, age, vocation and vacations, their friends, associates and most critically, it contained the badge stamp icon. Think gleaming portraits of the same hurried workers who walked the streets obscured and hidden and who went through every day without touching another human being, smiling with bright well-lit faces.

Rico was no different. He went though every day crouched under a portable badge station updating it while hiding his face. Like most, he lived in fear of the errant photo taken from a portable station that could capture a face in the background while focusing on a humorous advertisement, a cute animal, or a beautiful sky. These pictures, once saved, floated around until someone recognised the face and identified the badge portal, which even if the poor soul was able to remove the errant identification from his or her shining badge portal, the meta data remained, permanently. So the perfect portraits were at constant risk of being contaminated by an altogether different reality. One that most people, like Rico, did not want to world to see.

The badge was a prison of information, permanently attached. The badge was immortal.

As Rico refreshed his badge portal with the message "the 6 train is crazy today!" sitting down on a busy subway car, he glanced up just in time to see two men engaged in a struggle over a leather bag. Both wore the sort of linen face obfuscations that had become fashionable, or rather, desired. Although he often lurked in darkness, Rico didn't wear a mask. While he work his waxed jacket collar up and hid his face behind it with his hat pulled low, mask-free, he considered himself a rebel.

He wore only a low-slung hat. He did not, or so he thought, wear a mask even though he was just as frightened of metadata as the next man.

"Let go of my bag asshole!"
"Fuck you! This is my bag!"

Sensing trouble, passengers hurriedly updated their badge portals. The data would be aggregated and the police monitoring algorithms would notice the trends, subject matter and location of the messages. They knew that within a minute the train's camera feeds would be monitored and there would be an officer waiting at the next stop (or the one after that) by the specific door of their compartment.

The men were both large but one was muscular and larger than the other. He wore a grey business suit with a yellow tie with a bag that appeared to accessorise with his wardrobe. His hair, peaking out from his linen face cover, had just begun to gray. The other man wore ragged clothes. His shirt was ripped and his jeans had dirt and mud scruff markings. He was rail thin and his arms appeared sore and beaten. His shoes were ragged boots with no shoestrings, and a worn yet polished old leather briefcase. Despite this and the improbable nature of such a visibly disheveled man owning such a handsome bag, he seemed the most insistent that it was his.

Rico thought the dirty man must be attempting to rob the evidently wealthy man and that his insistence was because of hunger. People were snapping photos with their badge portals and refreshing with running commentary. The men were thrusting back and forth trying to pry the bag out of each other's hands. The train sped through the darkened tunnels throwing them off-balance so that they bounced back and forth against the plastic walls along the last benches before the exits. They nearly knocked over an elderly woman who rushed into the aisles. A few people shouted caution, but already moved to violence, the men ignored all pleas for reason and continued their struggle for the bag.

The well-dressed man in the grey business suit landed on the subway floor with a thud. His linen face cover nearly fell off. The silence was a warning after as the sound of his heavy mass hitting the floor because it announced the crossing of a new threshold of violence. He fixed his linen face mask and glared at the ragged man, who stood, clutching the bag, glancing around the car, in a nearly audible and desperate plea for help.

No one came and the heavy mass of rage clumsily picked himself up, swaddling on the clear barrier and lunged at the ragged man, striking him solidly in the head. A cascade of audible sighs filled the subway. The dirty man collapsed and red, rich blood flowed through his mask. He began to seize uncontrollably and the other man relentlessly kicked him in his abdomen. The dirty man appeared to be dying, dying and convulsing.

It was being refreshed and photographed in real time.

The door opened. There were no policemen. Would-be passengers standing on the crowded platform at Central Square saw the shaking man and the brutal hulking, well-dressed figure kicking him and stepped back from the closing doors. No one exited or entered. The large man was unforgiving. He continued to kick the dirty, convulsing and seizing man.

"Come on man! He's done!" Rico, cowardly, half-shouted in a weak voice, while crouching behind another passenger. He was afraid of any real confrontation but frightened even more by the violence, which in the context of the world as he knew it, was horrific to witness.

"What!" the well-dressed monster screamed to no one in particular. He had started to perspire from violent exertion. "Who said that?" No one responded. Rico pulled his hat lower and furiously updated his badge along with many other passengers. *Where were the police?* He wanted to do more but felt useless. After hearing no response, the well-dressed beast kept kicking and smiling. The ragged man had stopped convulsing and now was only a formless collection of clothes, sitting in a pool of dark red.

"That's enough" came a strong voice from the back. Just as the large man turned around to confront the strong voice, the doors opened. They were at another stop, 88th Avenue. There were no police there. Passengers-to-be standing on the platform again saw the commotion and declined to enter the train. This time, those standing behind the view of the violent man, rushed off the train. The well-dressed man again searched for the source of the second, more insistent voice of protest. Rico was trapped as the voice came from behind him and the large man blocked his path to the exit. He hoped that whichever brave soul had intervened was prepared to defend his words with more.

As the doors closed again, a hand came through and they reopened. It was the police. They came on board, several officers with large shades and hats grabbed the suit and in the scuffle his mask nearly came off. "No! Not my badge!" he screamed as he was led off by the two helmeted officers.

Rico leaned over to check on the scruffy, still man. Surrounded by an increasing pool of warmth, mixing with the dirt and excrement on the subway floor and growing cold, was the actual bare face of a man. He looked tired and afraid; his eyes wide open, gazing up.

People started gathering around and taking pictures.

To every true friend I have ever had, especially GK.

One's self I sing—a simple, separate Person;
Yet utter the word Democratic, the word En-masse.

Of Physiology from top to toe I sing;
Not physiognomy alone, nor brain alone, is worthy for the muse—I say the
Form complete is worthier far;
The Female equally with the male I sing.

Of Life immense in passion, pulse, and power,
Cheerful—for freest action form'd, under the laws divine,
The Modern Man I sing.

-Walt Whitman, Leaves of Grass, 1855.

Book 1

1.

In this house.

The only building in this congested, dark, masked, cloistered city where anyone felt free enough to walk around unmasked was, ironically, the home of what created the desire to hide and the place where that desire was strongest.

It was the home of the badge, a cavernous glass-encased cube centering on a lovely green park. During its construction, this indoor garden was marketed as a marvel. People came from other nations to sit in it and feel the unique way this modern structure enveloped the streets, contoured, and combined past and future. In reality the centre of this glass cube was just a park with a glass ceiling surrounded by a series of reinforced buildings that had been constructed to appear contiguous. There were several glass office blocks with a translucent material covering the courtyard in the centre. Each building sat side-by-side, separated by clear walls.

If you stood in the centre of this park and looked around, what you saw was a wonder of colours, people moving and working, light, activity, all interconnected. But while the buildings appeared open, unobstructed, the very essence of a post-modern world, unencumbered with the rigidity of the past, in reality they were nothing but a series of glass tunnels and walls that were impenetrable without immense power, literally and figuratively. Standing in the centre, looking outwardly at all of the floors and rooms, it seemed as if one could move from one floor to another with ease, talking and consulting, learning and growing along the way. In reality, each floor represented a stratum of power that took years to ascend.

Deep inside this complicated, seemingly transparent fortress was the office of the Central Monitor or Mon for short. His office was a series of glass rooms but within the inner sanctum, he sat in what was essentially a wood paneled closet, where often he wrote instructions under a desk lamp by hand. Whereas the creators and defenders of the system he presided over insisted that it symbolised openness, collaboration, transparency, to him, the overseer, it represented some of the most putrid aspects of humanity. Millions outside the cube wore masks while those inside wore nothing but pretended that the bright smiling photos that the world saw were real whereas, to him, the photos were another example of the artificiality and vanity of power. He knew none of it was real because he knew cameras and mirrors create actors out of human beings. He knew that when one's entire life is caught on camera, the acting takes on new dimensions of deception, inward and outward.

This is why he chose to sit inside a wooden closet alone in his thoughts, away from the machinery, buttons and lights. He knew that the cube was nothing but a warren of cameras, security sensors, gates, and people. On most days he didn't leave the closet unless he had a meeting, which was always in one of the series of glass rooms outside his office unless, that is, the President requested a meeting. He was powerful enough to make anyone else come to the cube.

Today, however, he journeyed to the grassy centre for a ceremony to honour employees that had won awards.

Because it was a public event, he had to dress in full uniform, emblazoned with medals and trinkets, and accompanied by a full retinue of junior officials. They were all arrayed on a platform in the centre facing dozens of employees. Standing behind them were hundreds of jumping and waving wives, husbands, sons and daughters, snapping photographs of the wall of brass, the glass kaleidoscope and the lovely trees. It was a beautiful day.

After the anthems, the introductions and applause, the employees filed by the wall of brass to shake the hands of all the officials. At the end, he handed each a certificate and thanked them for their service. He paused for photos with the bouncy children, aging parents or well-scrubbed adolescents that stood in a separate line waiting for their loved one to meet the Mon. After the flash, handshake, sometimes embrace, he turned and went to the next employee and family.

It was a graduation ceremony of sorts in the sense that each person waved their certificate proudly, their families gathered around, excited about the photo that would be placed on their badge portal with the Mon, a photo taken at the centre of the system with the most powerful man within the system, in an artificial park under a bright, shining sun.

It disgusted him that people could be so proud of a moment he regarded as deceitful, bound in a lie. These people, their families, treated it as an achievement, working and perpetrating something that was false. He sometimes wondered if it was only him or if all powerful men and women shared this cynicism at the joys and happiness of the people they led.

After the ceremony, it was a tradition for the Mon to tour the back office suites, where men in uniforms toiled in the forgotten manual labors, cooking, cleaning, the things that were often overlooked but still necessary in the age of computers, programmers and glass walls.

He gave a short laudatory speech and went into the back of one of the glass blocks followed by his mandatory retinue of security and junior officials. They gave him a white gown emblazoned with his name and title and goggles and he posed with workers doing things like sweeping floors, taking apart machines, and stirring massive pots of soups for the lunch canteen.

During one of these photo ops in the mailroom, the supervisor showed him some of the strange correspondence addressed to him that they had received during the past month. Cameras clicked and uniformed workers stood around watching as he laughed at the handwritten cartoons from children or the pasted letters from printed articles from the unhinged. He received, he was informed, hundreds of letters from the paranoid, the deluded, hysterical, supportive, obsessed, on a monthly basis that had to be screened and tracked. On a table spread out sat some of the more strange ones. There was one letter that caught his eye. It was in type print.

"What does that letter read?" He asked in a jovial mood. "Type print! Who has a typewriter these days!" More laughter, more cameras, as he picked up the letter.

He later decided that the letter arrived via an unorthodox route: the regular hand delivered postal mail. The only messages people sent using hand carriers were sentimental ones, invitations, post cards, holiday greetings, and even these sentimental occurrences justifying something so out of the ordinary, save for the occasional fad, were increasingly rare. This letter, however, was no exercise in nostalgia. It was functional, powerful, provocative, and it arrived in a filthy crumpled envelope bearing a postmark from Chad.

It took the letter three days from that initial glance to reach his hands, where he could really study its words, alone in his closet, and by that time it was taped together and sealed in plastic, seemingly so as to not contaminate the evidence. The beaten envelope had been brushed for prints (futile), the paper type analysed, the postmarks screened, and most importantly the actual letter, a letter written not in font but in typeface, an obscure typeface produced only by a typewriter last manufactured in New Jersey seventy-five years ago, yet here it was in a letter in a dirty envelope from Chad. The letter read:

> *We will destroy the quandary that bedevils us.*
> *For, although mysterious, we know how it operates*
> *In this house, we believe life is precious.*

> *XFGH001+--12*

The typeface was called Clearface. It was one of the first ever developed.

Standing now in front of the cameras, it was the last line that frightened him. He immediately recognised it as an equation from an outdated, derelict programming language they had used to build the first monitoring paradigm over twenty years ago. The equation itself was meaningless but within this context, the purposeful words, unconnected in even the slightest way to any electronic paradigm, must be viewed as a threat.

He quickly lost his jovial mood and threw the plastic envelope containing the letter back onto the table. "Who screened this letter and why is it on this desk?" he asked matter-of-factly. The room, full of security, officials, uniformed employees, grew still as everyone looked around, hoping that the person responsible would identify himself. Like a spotlight, attention and glares were directed to a chubby uniform standing to the side. He was the duty manager of the mailroom. The Mon, seeing everyone turn in his direction, looked directly at him. The man's face began to fill.

The senior official in charge of the mailroom function, who was standing next to the Mon, embarrassingly tried to intervene as the poor worker turned bright red and stumbled over his words.

"Mr. Monitor sir, I, I, I was, I . . . I" the clerk stuttered.

"Mr. Monitor, he is just discussing some crazy letters we receive from time to time, isn't that right Belvin?" the senior official said.

"Yeah, ah, yes sir, that's right" the clerk said, turning his head down and away.

"Yes, I understand young man. Look at me." The clerk looked up. "Describe this letter." The clerk described the letter in greater detail as the senior official nervously stood by.

"Bring this letter to Radcliffe. Radcliffe, where are you? There you are. Come here."

A tall slender man with a heavy beard casually walked from behind the cameras where he was watching the unfolding drama. Radcliffe was the Assistant Monitor, or AsMon for short.

"Excuse me ladies and gentlemen, we appear to have an issue here. Could you kindly for a moment leave us in the room to consult? Yes that's it, everyone out, except you and you" he said pointing to the senior official and duty manager. Everyone except the security left the room. The two others stood over the table wondering whether they would still be employed following what would happen next.

"Yes sir, what seems to be the issue?" Radcliffe asked, barely able to contain his irritation at the inexplicable delay.

"This young man screened this letter. Collect this letter. It sounds like it could be from one of these paradigm counterproductive-types." The air went out of the room and the two other men visibly flinched. Counterproductives were those who constantly threatened the viability of the badge, sometimes violently. There were a few sophisticated and well known counterproductive organizations. These groups often broke into their paradigms and stole information or disrupted operations and were the bane of modern society's existence. They prevented trains from running, street lights from functioning properly, cars from knowing where to go, bills from being processed, generally chaos, and because of the loss of life they caused, it was lawful for the Central Committee to treat them as combatants.

"Sir, our intelligence just doesn't reflect that conclusion. If that was the case we would have immediately escalated it to your office and we certainly wouldn't have left it on a table in full public view. This is just a stupid letter written by a crazed person!" The guard outstretched his hands in a waving angry motion but soon realised his lapse of decorum and regained his tone. The senior official interjected, giving the clerk a *'you're fired'* look. "Or maybe someone wasn't doing their job properly. In any event, I apologise at even getting you invo-"

"This young man has done nothing wrong. Do not discipline him. Just give Radcliffe the letter. Radcliffe, investigate it thoroughly." And with that the Mon left the room, picking back up his entourage of journalists and retinue of junior officers and they headed towards the workshop where the men who tended to the plants in the centre park worked.

Radcliffe was handed the letter by the shaking left hand of the senior official. He took the letter without a word and stuffed it into his jacket. He instructed them to report to his desk an hour later and headed off behind the Mon.

"I'm sorry sir. We had to tape the envelope back together." The senior official said a hour later standing before Radcliffe's desk. The duty manager was hanging his head sadly. "We did the best we could. It's still in good shape. I don't think it's from a counterpro but there it is." Radcliffe continued to read the screen implanted on his desk as if the senior official wasn't there. "Sir, I mean, I mean . . . , sir, is there, I mean, is there anything else we can do?" Radcliffe looked up and towards the door.

The men backed out of his office into an ornate lobby. The senior official slapped the head of the clerk and cursed him as they walked into the AsMon's private elevator manned by a large security guard. They had never been inside the executive column, didn't even have the security clearance and were too nervous to notice the gilded paintings, the dark wooden tables with monitors built right in, the ancient carpets and so on. They had to win a contest to even be able to get in the same room as the Mon and AsMon. Being in the presence of the AsMon was terrifying enough but doing so under these circumstances was enough to make any man quaver, especially one who worked for the Worldwide Data Security Cooperative (WDSC) or the Coop, whichever you prefer.

While the two men were nervously providing him the letter, Radcliffe was browsing through their entire life histories, their parents, their interests, their phone conversations, the phone conversations of their closest friends and associates, to see if anything was interesting. One of them, the manager, was the child of immigrant parents from Sweden, so while he stood shaking before him, Radcliffe executed a request to the Swedish data house and obtained information on his parents almost seamlessly. Everything, everyone it seemed, was connected.

He picked up the dirty envelope with a pencil and shook out the letter, placing latex gloves on before spreading it out. He read the letter three times but didn't see any significance or most importantly, any reason why the Mon would be so interested. This actually caused him some anxiety. Besides running the WDSC, his other job was to keep the Mon happy. Something about this letter bothered him and Radcliffe intended to find out.

He had it fingerprinted, traced, researched, placed under infrared lighting, all over a period of two days and couldn't identify any reason why the Mon would think this had anything to do with a gnat or counterpro. He knew it was written on an old typewriter in an old typeface and that it contained a really old piece of programming language but this didn't seem particularly noteworthy.

Finally, he went to see the Mon and present his findings.

The Mon's office was even more elaborate, a series of six conference and meeting rooms, each with large projectors blanketing the walls surrounding the latest in desk visual equipment. Three of the rooms seemed to be constant hubs of activity. Young aides scurried in and out exchanging ideas on flat screens images projected over the tables and consulting with foreign data houses over the projector screens on the walls. Normally when he walked into an office, people stopped and watched but not in the Mon's suite. The aides ignored him and continued to work.

He walked through the bustling rooms until he got into the private suite of the Mon (one he hoped he would occupy one day). Sitting at his desk before the Mon's door was his private secretary Daniel. He always struck Radcliffe as someone who wasn't cut out for the Coop, anxious, jumpy, reactionary and ostensibly more loyal to the Mon than the organization.

"Hi Daniel."
"Hello Radcliffe!" Daniel said, looking up from a retro desktop monitor.
"Is he in? I need to speak to him about something urgent."

"Yes yes, right this way." Daniel got up and opened the door. "He's been waiting on you. Your administrator updated your status."

"I figured" Radcliffe said as he walked into the Mon's office.

It wasn't really an office. Instead of the expansive office suite surrounded on two sides by a balcony with views of the monuments, he chose what had been before a storage closet. He still used the large office for formal meetings but meetings with the AsMon weren't usually formal. There were only two chairs surrounding a metal frame table with the latest greatest desk device sitting on top. He was busily scribbling and typing something onto it.

"Sir, I have something for you." Radcliffe said as he held out the letter.

"What is this?" he asked, not reaching for it.

"It's that letter from a few days ago. You know the one you overheard the mail clerk discussing and asked that I look into it."

"Oh that thing, hmm, well what have you found?"

"Nothing much, unconnected."

"Totally?" he asked looking up.

"Completely sir. But that's the only thing interesting about it. Whoever sent it used an old typeface and an old typewriter, not surprising given it came from a rural African country." He looked back down at his screen.

"Give it to Daniel. That will be all."

"Thank you sir. I will leave my report with him as well?"

"Yes, thanks Radcliffe."

"You're welcome sir." Radcliffe lingered standing above the table for a few seconds. The Mons looked up awkwardly and impatiently.

"Yes Radcliffe?" he asked annoyed.

"Sir, well, I am just wondering. I've been your assistant for a number of years now. We know pretty much everything about one another but I guess I don't really know you. How about we have lunch one of these days?"

"Radcliffe, I am going to recommend that you replace me when I retire. Do you have anything else for me? I am really busy preparing for my testimony before Congress."

"No sir. No that will be all." Radcliffe smiled to himself as he walked out of the room and slammed the letter and report on Daniel's desk.

"I love you too!" Daniel shouted after him.

"What was that about sir?" Daniel asked, turning back into the Mon's office.

"Oh nothing, Radcliffe trying to endear himself to me." He did a gagging motion and Daniel laughed gratuitously as if what he said was funny.

"So funny sir."

"Yes I know. Listen. Daniel take those files Radcliffe left you and do some background and convene a meeting with some of the assistants. Let me know so I can attend."

Three hours later he was sitting around a table with the best and brightest the nation had to offer discussing the implications of a dingy letter from Africa.

"This is Chad after all. I mean they don't even have satellite connectivity. Can we really be afraid of a gnat system in a country without sat connectivity?" one particularly brilliant young analyst intoned. He listened to the room agree with the brilliant analyst for a couple minutes before weighing in. His thoughts kept returning to the series of numbers at the end of the letter, the old equation. If the sender had this equation, could they have others, the next revision, and the next language?

"The author is too smart to send it from the country where he is based. We should focus on bordering or nearby countries with sufficient technological infrastructure."

The room grew quiet. No one had thought of this.

Then it came to him, the reason why he recognised the series of numbers out of the corner of his eyes, why he asked Radcliffe to look into it, why he instantly knew this letter would mean something to him.

"On second thought, actually let's just drop this. You're right. Even if it isn't Chad, none of the bordering nations have sat connectivity either. We're wasting our time. Surely, it would take sat connectivity to threaten our systems. Where are we on the China consultation?" The aides sprang to life and pulled up presentations on the wall screens. He casually picked up the letter and threw it in the trash.

After the meeting, he told all of them to go home early and paused before leaving the room. "Actually let me hold on to this," he said reaching into to the small trashcan for the crumpled letter. It has value to me. I haven't seen this typeface since I was a boy."

"Typeface? What's that?" One of the smart alecs joked, receiving a rowdy response. He patted him on the back and smiled, walked back to this office and closed the door. Everyone wondered why he chose to work in a storage closet after reaching the pinnacle of achievement and obtaining the office everyone in town wanted. But it was the only room in his suite where it was difficult to place high frequency cameras and microphones. Even though he was the boss, this storage closet was the only place he had privacy from the organization he ran, built, and structured.

He burst into loud sobs. The sequence of numbers at the end was the first piece of code he ever learned from the most genius programmer he ever met and the only man he ever loved. It was a message to him. He held the stained envelope to his face and tried to breathe in his scent, imagine where he was, what he looked like these days. Tears started to soak the envelope, melting the postmarks and address into a blurry cloud of ink. He couldn't get a smell and he cried from a deep place of isolation and longing.

The letter was written to him by his brother.

2.

Across the reflection.

Across a specious space, they looked day and day, never any closer than the three-foot table that divided them, meaningless yet insurmountable. Her name was Elizabeth and she was his best friend, or at least he liked to pretend. They worked in the same division. She had light brown eyes like his mother. He knew how to make her laugh. She knew how to make him smile. They ate meals privately. He had seen where she lived. They could touch each other, comfortably, on the shoulder, the hands.

They had full access to each other's badges.

But they were no closer than friends. The table represented the permanency of the gulf and the intimacy of their relationship. It was there everyday, only a few feet wide. And yet it was there every day, only a few feet thick. She even resembled his features. She could have been his sister. He found himself wanting to say

> *"Elizabeth, I love you. I love you as if you were a part of my physical body, not infatuation but love, the kind that is more like need or depend. I love you."*

But he never secured the courage and never forgave or forgot the angst. So they continued in the same way, in perpetuity, with her telling him everything, about her latest celebrity or celebrity-seeking boyfriend, how grand (or hideous) he behaved and yet showing little interest in *his* stories, mainly fictional, about his romance. At those, and this moment, he could only love her anyway so he didn't mind. The dates and stories were mainly of desperation, loneliness and hope that either he could finally say "I love you" and she would reply "I love you too" or that his heart would just let go, that he would find another sister with light brown eyes just like mama; because, everyone has dreams.

Unpacking a ham sandwich, unsettled by the day's earlier events, he looked across the table and nervously asked "what do you see when you see me?" Her hair was frazzled today. She had started wearing it out and at times it got bushy. The darkness of her hair was a compliment to her skin, he thought. She was unwrapping a plastic container of lettuce, tomatoes and carrots.

"I see a nice guy." She said nonchalantly before glancing up from the container with a puzzled expression. "Why?"
Her words stung. He saw something so meaningful in her, eyes, hair, smile, how could he just be a "nice guy" to her and how could she wonder or be confused why he wanted to know what the mirror reflected.

He stopped asking questions like these a while ago when he accepted that she wasn't in love with him. Her answers always depressed him but today he was more anxious and curious.

"I saw a man killed on the train today and instead of helping, most people were more concerned with their badges, their photo being taken. They curled up and hid from the light, including me. I'm wondering right now who am I? What am I? What are we?"

She looked at him with a blank stare. There was no sign of emotion.

"Uhhh, first your name is Rico, second you like guitar" she replied sarcastically.

"Elizabeth, I know all that. I'm being serious here. I know who I am but I want to know *who I am*. Don't you see?"

She looked confused now and opened her eyes wide, confused under a glow of natural light. She also was radiant and beautiful, confused, smart, beautiful, confused.

"My boyfriend was saying something similar. You know he's really into that new show Serendipity. All the guys who work at the White House you know, his friends, are into it. Last night's episode was about that. Chris Lewis, the lead, was standing on the Statute of Liberty screaming 'Who am I?' Hehehe, you're like him, on Serendipity, hehehe."

He wanted to violently throw something at her, but just rolled his eyes.

"Elizabeth, when I see you, I see me. We're so much alike but sometimes I believe you don't want to see the same thing in me, that is why you know, why . . ."

"Why what? You're my friend."

"I'm not hungry." He pushed his food forward and moved his chair back. "Here's some chips. You like this kind."

"But why . . . why are you leaving?"

"Elizabeth I saw a man die today, which presented me with a deep existential challenge that I'm having difficulty reconciling with all this bullshit, the ham sandwich, these omnipresent badges and talking about a 'famous' boyfriend you have nothing in common with except that he's everything you wish you were and me, when you look at me, I'm everything you wish you weren't."

"Excuse me?"

"You hate yourself. You hate me. But you, we, can't really hate ourselves, or at least that's really hard to do actively so we create fake selves, fake happiness, and we duck anytime someone brings out the camera to catch us with our masks down."

He was standing now. The break room, usually empty except for them, had a window that faced out into the bright afternoon sky. He wanted to touch that light, be in it, but he knew that if he looked outside the window he would see nothing but a mass of office buildings.

"We're not compatible. You're not my type." she said defensively but off in space away from him. He had heard those words before so many times in many different contexts that he had come to believe them, accept them, as a strategy to make himself believe there was a reason why the table always remained.

"Elizabeth, I . . . I . . . I'm just a little shaken up today." He turned to walk away.

"But what if you want more than what you see?" she said softly, still staring off into space.

"Huh?"

"What if you don't hate yourself but just want more to, you know, be happy?"

"But why can't you be happy with what you have? Why must one want something different or as you phrase it, more?"

"Sometimes in the mirror, you know, there are all kinds of ideas and thoughts, some would say scars tied up in what we see. Sometimes the best way to cope is to seek a different reflection. It's not hate. I guess it can be called escape."

"You can escape in love." he whispered under his breadth.

"What was that?" she asked, engaged.

"Nothing, it was nothing. I need to be alone. Please have these chips. They're your favorite."

He walked out of the break room into a deserted hallway and back to his office, closed the door and put his face in his hands, waiting for the inevitable tears. "Why couldn't he tell her?" he thought. He felt like such a failure. He eyes started moistening as the thought of holding her in love was becoming an impossible fantasy, one that he had not done enough, he felt, to realise even though he was only three feet away from it every day.

And then he heard a loud "BEEP" sound.

He looked up. Someone had sent him a private badge message. It read "Come see me. I have something for you."

3.

Into the safe place.

He walked a couple kilometers until he was off the well-paved and orderly roads until he reached more crowded, chaotic, broken pavements.

The only person he told was Daniel and the few facts given were intended to obscure his real destination. Usually when he told Daniel he needed a "time out" it meant some exotic location with exotic company. Daniel arranged the papers and electronic cover, placement of his modules at his work retreat, manipulation of the identification and persona of some real but oblivious participant, normally an elderly person who had few connections, and of course wasn't on the badge. Daniel secured for him also new phones, which included everything, payment mechanisms, identifications, location and messaging services and of course a telephone, digital.

He left the digital devices, the identification, and the faux participant IDs, and everything else on a boat in the Indian Ocean, floating 200 yards off an island known locally as Paeikaana Theevukal in the middle of the Maldives, at the center of Paeikaana Theevukal sat an ageing thatched-roof cottage surrounded by ancient palms. In the small kitchen, wrapped in newspaper underneath the floorboards underneath the oven were another set of identification documents along with large amounts of Chinese currency placed there years earlier, before he tucked the newspaper package inside his pants and caught a ride on a rusty fishing craft manned by a few workers he flagged down with a large smoking palm branch. He got the boat to take him to Colombo and eventually, after a circuitous route through three continents, with no payment mechanism, no luggage, wearing a wig and occasionally shades, he arrived on this bustling and claustrophobic street with hundreds, if not thousands staring as he walked down the street before hailing a beaten, filthy, multi-colored thing ominously labeled "Yellow" cab.

The airport had been modern, just like all the ones in Europe. It seemed constructed by the same people, the movements, machines, cameras, security, or was he being paranoid? Yes. He was but he needed to be. By doing this, he was risking more than, albeit nearly over, his career, and his life. He was risking the entire project.

From the airport, his hotel provided a shuttle that took him down a well-manicured highway. Someone had taken great care to ensure that there was no trash along the main road. The highway took him across a wide, beautiful bridge constructed to avoid the congestion of local roads. The shuttle driver had to pay a toll to use it; "complimentary" for guests of course he said smiling as he handed over paper notes to the toll attendant.

The road weaved through a glistening, glass embossed business district before reaching a series of waterfront hotels and residences. The shuttle stopped in a red brick parkway that circled around a lighted fountain in front of his hotel. He exited into a lobby encircled with wall-to-floor screens alternating great postmodern works of art. It was beautiful and posed an almost existential contrast with the chaos he had witnessed outside. He wanted to recoil.

There were monitors, scanners, guests with modules, giddy young people at the restaurant inside and outside on the walkway snapping photos and updating their badges. After checking in, putting down a fake payment mechanism and identification, he found a magnificent room looking over the lagoon. He could see yachts and smaller boats dotting in and out of the lagoon to the sea. 'What a beautiful place this is' he thought.

Taking most of his cash, shades and adjusting his wig, he walked out of the lobby where an eager and frightened concierge attempted to stop him from walking down the red brick parkway. "Sir!" he said, "you cannot walk. Look at how busy the road is with trucks and cars. There are no sidewalks here."

He pushed him aside to the shock and horror of the other staff and guests standing in the lobby, walked along the well-paved roads until he was far enough away that even the well-dressed concierge felt anxious at following him until he discovered the putrid cab.

Inside, it smelled like old urine and sweat. The backseat was covered with dirty towels. He told the driver a fake address on the other side of the city and got a suspicious and cautious glance. Most drivers were sharks when it came to gullible foreigners who asked to go to slums and normally the driver wouldn't take people to that area. It was bound to be a set up, going that far. But, because he had partially grew up in the area and because the man was a foreigner who he felt a patronizing tinge of sympathy for, he decided to take him. If something happened to this weird polite man with the funny shades and wig he would feel guilty.

The roads and scenery got progressively grimmer. They crossed back over the water on a long bridge, but a different, toll free bridge. There was no manicured highway where they were going.

Beggars knocked on the windows; trash was everywhere, as far as the eye could see. Open sewers flowed with disgusting symphonies of colors and smells, and people, walking riding, standing, sitting, filled every conceivable frame.

Children, some naked, and seemingly wretched with no supervision, walked through the trash-strewn streets alone. As they pushed deeper and deeper into the maze of streets and bodies, the homes relegated to cinder block fixtures, some with no roof. The roads became flooded grand rivers with hidden rocks that threatened to overturn the taxi when it jammed one.

More than once he saw dead bodies rotting alongside the road. 'What a horrible place this is' he thought, shrinking back into his seat.

But he knew exactly where he was and he was determined. He had asked a research intern to bring him a book of paper maps from every continent, even though he only needed one. "Why?" the intern had asked. "We have all them in the paradigm. I can have them project any of them on this wall here or even sent to your eyeglass monitor."

"It's a habit of mine," he replied. "I'm kind of old-fashioned."

So when they got to their destination, a congested highway overpass overlooking a massive market packed with what seemed to be over a million souls, he asked the driver to stop. The driver looked back, expecting payment, instead he told him to take him to another location entirely outside the town.

"Sir! That is in an entirely different region. There is no way I could drive you there and back before dark!"

"I know, I understand. I want you to stay with me overnight. I will pay you." The driver's eyes started darting and he squirmed nervously.

"Sir, it is dangerous on those roads. I don't feel it is safe. I have a family. I need to return tonight."

"Very well then, thank you for your time and effort. Here is what I owe you" he said handing the driver a thick wad of bills and walking off into the crowds. The driver looked at the wad of crisp bills as they soaked up the moisture in his sweating hands and then back at the foreigner with the wig who was getting mobbed by beggars and trying to shoo them away.

"Sir! Sir! Come back, I will help you!" he screamed desperately, pushing through the crowd and nearly knocking over several beggars and grabbing the man by the shirt. "Come back to my cab. It is not safe for you to be here alone." They got back into the car and pushed on. Nightfall was a short time away and the skies were beginning to darken.

But he wasn't afraid because he knew where they were. They entered a highway clogged with trucks, some of them broken down blocking traffic, others packed with dozens of people sitting with blank stares as if they were animals being taken to slaughter. Sometimes they had to swerve mightily to avoid gaping holes in the highway. Other times when traffic slowed, they had to be careful as to not crush the young children, some who looked as young as five, that were darting between the tight spaces hawking water and snacks.

"If we kill one, we cannot stop because they will lynch us," the driver announced with the pride of a tour guide. Still, occasionally they passed through serene bush, quiet with few other people or cars in sight, poignant and moving under the setting sun. Before long they entered another crowded and hustling city. It was dusk now and the driver turned on his lights and pulled into what appeared to be yet another slum. After driving only a few hundred yards they were stopped at a checkpoint manned by loud young men, some of whom banged the car making ominous threats and demanding money.

He looked around. It was hard to see as there were no street lights, few lights in any of the cinderblock houses, yet he could feel the humanity walking to and fro on the street and he could make out a corner and a light-colored house ahead. He got out of the car and the yelling, seemingly violent men paused and watched the foreigner get out and casually walk away. He walked a few feet, squinted at the house and walked back and gave the driver half of his money. "Go home" he told him directly. The driver, exhausted, frustrated and out of patience, looked around at the young men salivating at the foreigner who had just flashed a year's wages in cash and jumped back into the dirty cab and put it in reverse. He would find a hotel before things got ugly.

The men, however, didn't rob him. One of them scanned him, unsure what to do. Foreigners never came here, except for . . . The formerly violent man approached him cautiously. He was looking around, trying to get his bearing. The leader put this hand out in a calm manner.

"Can we help you sir?" the young man asked. His articulate and polished accent seemed incompatible with his sweat-soaked, ragged exterior.

"No. I know where I am and where I am going." He marched off to the fading white house directly ahead down the rain soaked and flooded street. It was difficult to see where the pot holes were.

"But sir," the articulate man protested, followed by the other stunned members of his group "You are surely here to see Sogi, the foreigner that lives here or why else would you come here."

He looked at the young man critically. He knew so much about him, only by looking at his appearance.

"And if I were looking for this Sogi?"

"Well sir, if you were then you made a wrong turn. Sogi lives just up that hill there. In the pink brick house." The maps had directed him to the wrong house. The articulate man pointed to a cluster of cinder brick buildings off from the gravel road, one of which was painted a bright peach color. He was surprised. He thought he had all the information he needed and here he was totally lost and dependent on a man who didn't even have a telephone.

"Thank you. I will go there first," he said.

"No sir. Please. I will lead you."

He followed the young man, who was followed by the burgeoning group of other young men, most of whom had been on the verge of violently attacking his driver ten minutes prior.

For the first time he realised that there were a lot of mosquitoes. No one else seemed to mind but he felt like he was being ravished for dinner.

They arrived at the peach house and the young man knocked and waited for an answer before announcing something in a language he couldn't understand. The door opened and a hulking figure with a stern look came to the door exchanging words with his guide and then turning and looking the new guest up and down.

"You're welcome." The hulking muscular figure said and opened the door wide, revealing a series of dark corridors that the guide, grabbing his hand, led him through. He could hear the footsteps of the other men as they followed behind. They arrived at a room that appeared to be in the back of the house, which was lit only by a lantern. There were at least 20 people crammed into the sweltering room, not to mention the others that had followed him inside.

Everyone was gathering around a lone figure that was reciting technical language. He was wearing a robe with what appeared to be prayer beads, and was instructing those gathered around him, in an evangelical-like type of sermon.

He recognised the voice. He could hear it in his mind, in his dreams, over and over, and now he heard it before him. The robed man looked up and their eyes met. It was his brother. When they made eye contact, his brother smiled. Behind a beard that seemed as if he hadn't been shaven in years and neatly groomed hair, he yelled joyfully "Welcome to Africa dear brother!" He threw his hands up in victory and raced to embrace him. They held each other until it hurt to do so. The crowded, almost praying young men, followers, students, prostrated on the ground before the robed man and their new guest.

4.

From the depths.

50 years ago, several miles below the surface of the rich, lush land, the earth moved, grinding, smooth, pink, orange, neon, molten, rock, fissures, chemical reactions, hard, force. Then, like a door slightly off hinge but pushed with fortitude, the friction passed and the rocks slid into place, closing seamlessly.

But the occurrence had released danger, forces, deep within the heart of our existence, that man was incapable of understanding.

There had been environmental disasters before, some man made, others God-born, some resolved through "science," invention, others through natural waves of cosmic change but for all of the world's advancement and knowledge, it often seemed that civilization was still composed of illiterate, half naked primitives worshipping the summer solstice.

The rich, lush, land was full of valleys, mistful mountains, rivers, deep vibrant trees dripping with fruit, exotic plants, animals and cream-coloured beautiful, the most beautiful, people, with wide knowing eyes. These people derived from one of the earliest cultures and they knew what they didn't know so most of them remained in the rich valleys and worked the land and worshipped in ancient temples to Zion, the religion that came from Jerusalem several thousand years prior.

But some went away and eventually obtained new knowledge, on topics as how to grow the old foods in new ways, new languages, beliefs, ways to use the land. These travelers introduced the people to foreign ideas, ways of seeing the world that many, tired of the antiquated colours, readily embraced.

This ancient civilisation erected new buildings, roads, dams, and completely transforming the rich, lush, land. Some refused to believe in this New Power and the lines that fed the lights in the bustling capital, and remained in the isolated valleys, but they were all interconnected, so the erosion from the stripped hills, the increased and decreased flows from the dammed river, affected the birds, the plants, the pools, even in the most remote of the rich, lush, land.

The magical, mysterious, reaction of molten molecules deep below the rich, lush, land, combined with this new knowledge and ways of doing, created something that, again, man was incapable of understanding or comprehending.

This was the story of the cream-coloured woman standing before an audience of eager listeners, some masked, some not, hidden in the basement of a bookstore.

First the pool below her grandmother's house, formerly filled with little delicious fish, and occasionally visited by wild game, foxes, deer and small primates, the lily of the valley, became a pond, a dirty salty pond that killed all the fish. The animals no longer arrived. Plants died. She was forced to walk several miles each days to get water where before the pool disappeared, all she had to do was run a few dozen metres, scoop a cupful of clear liquid and bring it to her Nana's lips.

Then the small pond became a lake, ever more filthy, salty, disgusting, forcing them to leave the land they had lived on for at least a century. Her Nana stopped speaking, mourning the lost of her Muheala, the name she gave the pool, which had sustained generations of her ancestors.

They moved into the nearest town, dirty, overcrowded, ten people sharing a single room. She had to queue for an hour for water now but at least the well, built by a foreign church, and was clean.

Then the filthy lake became what seemed like an ocean and the town had to be deserted. The community disbanded. Sometimes, the woman said, she mourned not only the lost of her grandmother, her Nana, who died the day before the they were placed on buses and sent to the capital, buried underneath that decrepit salty water that arose out of her Muheala, but just the ability to speak her language.

"My name is La Paz and this is my story." She said.

She sat down and the audience applauded. People began filing out, some after spending a few moments talking with her. She was cheerful and energetic. Rico waited patiently and eventually after most had left, he approached her cautiously.

"La Paz" he said looking down, "my name is-"

"Rico, your name is Rico" she said holding out her hands.

"How do you know who I am?"

"We organised this meeting and screened all of the attendees. I know who you are." She looked at him, un-frightened, unfazed, unafraid. He felt that they were alone in the room. "You visited our advocacy site. That's how we got your information." She nodded towards a shirking man with a notepad writing down contact information at a desk by the door. He rested his hands in hers.

"Paz, well, I wanted to say, you're very brave. To come and speak without a mask, to put your information in public. There must be several trackers in here but you still came and spoke. I really felt your story and I want to help you."

She smiled. Clasping her hands together away from his then touching his face lightly, she tugged at the cloth bandana. "It was true. Rico."

"What was true?"

"I do have something for you." She looked deep into his eyes. "Why do you wear this?" she asked puzzled.

"Well there are trackers here. I have a job. I admire your bravery and thank you for reaching out but I rather not go too public with-"

She snatched off his mask, revealing his face. He jerked back defensively, afraid, but she reached again for his face, touching him. He relaxed upon realising that everyone was gone except for her assistant at the door.

"Look at you. You look like my brother. You are beautiful, like the people of my homeland. I want to speak my language with you." She caressed the side of his face. He looked at her deeply, wondering, whether she was really of the same planet, the same plane, whether her story was real. She seemed real yet fantastical, exotic but authentic. She put her hands into his hair.

"You are beautiful. Why do you hide your face? Why are you afraid of what these people will think?"

5.

Brother.

He spent that night in a crowded room on top of old linoleum tiles, inches away from his brother where he could hear his breath and that of the dozen or so others smashed into this space. It reminded him of their childhoods sleeping in homeless dormitories, fighting for survival, parentless, adults by their teenage years.

He learned to fear kindness and respect brusqueness. Unlike the dormitory, where the night filled the air with mad screams, accusations and terrorisms, anxiety at being touched, here people laid on one another, packed tightly, sleeping in deep, close harmony. It was a place of peace and soon he drifted into a nether realm of sky, float, clouds.

He felt movement but was still in that purgatory between rest and awake, and when he finally did awake, the room was empty except for a few men sweeping the floor. The chaotic and bustling dormitory was now an empty room.

"Aburro, good morning" one man said cheerfully with a broom. "The others are outside. There is water for washing up and breakfast there." He then went back sweeping matter-of-factly.

Outside, he saw his brother engaging in what can only be described as half Yoga, half church service. He, of course, remembered that his brother was a Yoga instructor in many lives past. It was how they got off the streets and bought their first computing machine. To him, the Yoga was always a hustle to support their technological addictions but now he realised that it held much more meaning to his brother. Eyes closed, one leg raised and extended he stood in perfect balance, chiseled, seemingly deep in concentration, humming a rhythmic tone.

A group of men awkwardly tried to mimic him from behind, some better than others. He leaned against the cinderblock wall of the house and watched patiently. When his brother finished, a series of ever more difficult poses, he opened his eyes, kneeled, and mouthed some words, Holy, a prayer, and then gathered his small towel and shirt and walked away towards a row of buckets lined in the distance.

The terrain had distilled in the morning light. There were a cluster of corrugated tin roofed, cinderblock dwellings on top of a hill. You could see for miles in the distance, lightly covered red ground punctuated by other clusters every few miles and then a wide, white-capped river pushing through the group of scattered clusters to infinity. It was a marvelous sight.

He went to his brother who was washing his face.

"You still in the Yoga game I see brother?"
"Brother, you sleep okay?" He responded without turning around, his words muffled by the splashing water.

"Yes, not bad, for an un-air-conditioned shit hole in the jungle."

"You're too smart for that aburro. This is no jungle." These words came from a man next to his brother, one of the better Yoga practitioners. He was also splashing water on his face. "This aburro, is grassland." The men finished splashing their faces and others in line took their place. Drying his face and hair, his brother looked worriedly at the other man, who stood stern-faced and alert. The tension and faux anger in his face reminded him of the men down the hill who had banged on his taxi.

"Brother, meet William. They call him the Conqueror." His brother let out a giggle at the clever name play and slapped William on the back but William continued to stand, expressionless. "William, we will be back."

"Yes, Sir, but isn't aburro going to wash his face?"

"No William, we're going to walk down the back route to the river. He can wash there. Put the security on alert. Begin the first training session without me. Don't connect the machines. Just drill the code we discussed to the bogs on the dry erase board."

"Yes sir, right away!"

There was something uneasy about the way William went from anger to subservience in the flicker of a light, again, similar to the men down the hill.

His brother noticed his look of befuddlement and put his arm around him and led him away. They walked past other dwellings with children splashing their faces, women cooking food on outdoor fires, until they reached a dense palm grove.

"The Yoga wasn't a hustle brother. I made it seem like one to try and be cool to you and our friends but it changed my life, opened my eyes. I never told you but I fell in love with that hippy woman."

"She was 30 years older!" he shouted. In return, his brother looked at him with a sense of disappointment. He felt ashamed, as if there was some different, unique moral code to their lives that he just violated. He realised that the moral code he lived by everyday, the code of the badge, sometimes fooled him into thinking he actually believed it.

"I'm sorry. I'm very . . . that must have been bad." He looked away.
"Brother, it was. Before you leave, I have to tell you something very important. There's no time now. I just want to hear your voice for now on the shore of the creek.

He paused and they embraced. They both cried, free to express emotion openly for the first time since he arrived.

"Okay, okay, it's okay eh?" His brother said, regaining his parental control. He dried his brother's eyes with his faded cotton shirt. They continued down the narrow trail until it opened into a small clearing and a gushing rocky creek.

"Go on, wash your face. Drink the water even. It's very clean, for now." He kneeled on the creek bank and began to splash his face, finding the water very refreshing.

"I bet you're wondering why I'm here brother."

"Brother, I just wanted to ."

"No, it's fine. I know who you are and who you really are. I trust you. I knew you would come in peace. No one could ever replace my brother."

"That's right."

"I'm here because I believe what's happening in the world is wrong. I fell in love with the "data," with machines. I wrote the algorithm that has created this world and I hate it: I hate the world and I hate what you've become. Brother, join me. We can change it, the world."

He sounded like so many semi-wild delusional street preachers he encountered these days on the badge.

"I can't. I'm the . ."

"Aah, ho, hey, you would never join me. I felt I had to offer, like in the movies eh?" He finished washing his face. His brother took off his clothes and jumped into the creek swimming to the middle and reclining against a wide bolder. He remained on the creek bank with his shirt in his hands drying his face, watching his brother so relaxed, so happy, at peace.

"I'm holding them back brother."

"Holding who back?"

"You saw William? The flash of anger? I'm just a lid, all the Yoga shit, prayer, on a jar sitting on a fire."

"So it's still a game to you?"

"No, no game. I believe in it, without it, I couldn't do anything, least of all got all these angry, intelligent young men to believe."

"Why here? Believe what?" He was still confused.

"I'll never be able to answer those questions. That's what I was going to say, if you asked me why I'm here." He sighed deeply, eyes closed, still leaning on the white washed bolder. "There are practical reasons. It's off the grid. Your computers have a hard time finding me here. The government isn't friendly to the badge, for one, secondly, power is scarce, no data centres, no fucking algorithms. Those things require constant, reliable power. But the truth is, I don't know. The people are smart but poor so they make great programmers but there are a million other places I could've chose but I don't know. I love it here. The river, trees. What I love most is that this can feel like a desert yet one where everything grows."

"What do you hope to accomplish? You will never destroy the system, the badge. You will be killed."

"People used to tell me I couldn't build a company because I was from the streets, that I couldn't get investors because I spoke the language of the streets, that I couldn't change the world, that I couldn't disappear, that I couldn't heal sickness. My whole life has been about proving maxims like 'you can't' wrong."

"Ah I see, so it's about dismantling what you built, just to prove you can. It's about you."

"The egotistical component in me, you, it is, but to the man who gave up his wealth, his home, to spend years living in the dust, to feel children, build homes, to pray, sing, dance, to live, it's about something much deeper. The glory."

"I don't believe you. The only glory you want is for yourself."

"No. I'm not pretending anymore brother, like you. You aspired to your office because it was there, nothing more. I used to be like that but now, no, the only glory I see is the glory of God."

"God?"

"Yes, God. The fish that swim in this creek keep swimming until they reach the big river and keep swimming still until they reach the ocean. You dam the river, the birds that eat them and other animals die. These birds spread trees, eat rodents, soon this comes back to the village. More hunger, struggle, all from man playing God. The essence of God is harmony. I've discovered it."

"What does that have to do with the badge?"

"It's unnatural. Last time I was in the city I was sickened. People hiding, scared, cowering. What kind of world is that?"

"People don't hid. All information is available. That's the opposite of hiding."

"Listen to yourself brother. I bet you hide everyday. You had to hide to get here. What happened to the man with a guitar in the village square railing against his government, agitating for peace? That man is still here. That man is me." He opened his eyes and looked away. His brother was another anti-badge warrior. He had heard it a thousand times before.

"You think you know my type but you don't. I created the badge. I know the analytics. I can connect the dots. That's why these people are angry."

"I don't understand."

"If you travel 31 miles upriver from the large town, they are building that dam to power a data centre hundreds of miles further away, just to make the algorithm run a few milliseconds faster. This village will be flooded, only the hilltop will remain but it will be uninhabitable.

"It's not only for the badge. That power will drive industry in this area, create jobs."

"Semantics. You think this technology is just about hiding your face but it's disharmony. You hide your face, you stop singing, it's just as destructive to the world if you dam up the rivers and kill the fish. Disharmony here leads to disharmony everywhere. It's unnatural, it's inhuman, and I will defeat it."

"You are one man with an jungle village!"

"Didn't you hear anything I said? I am one man intertwined, a child of God, with the world. My actions can set forth a chain of events. I am one man, true, but I'm also a vital link in the orchestra."

"So you're the conductor, hmm, you are the God you seek to praise?"

"God is the conductor."

"You're not the first megalomaniac savior to the world."

"And I won't be the last." He dove into the water, staying for a minute, before coming out to the shore, exhaling and breathing deeply. "Brother, I know you would never come here to stay but I'm happy here and for the first time in my life I began to struggle with the consequences of what I've done years ago but I'm finally living truthfully. I don't have to lie and I know that if I die, my ideas will live on because they are harmonious and pleasing to God."

Smiling, he finally understood, responding "Brother, there will always be people like me, and people like you. Both of us are willing to kill, to destroy, for our aims. You think you're at peace with your trees, your creeks, but you're not at peace. You're at war."

He contemplated what he heard, smiled and kissed him on the cheek.

"Brother, you are wrong. I am at peace right here, right now, because you are here with me."

6.

Words belie.

The most basic equation, mathematical expression, is simply two factors on opposite sides of the sign for meaning. This, equals, that. (There are some equations and, some simple statements that can have meaning for life).

This equals that. Sun equals light. Night equals dark. Except that, life's equations are never as simple as words make them appear. Cold air equals beautiful fall days, crisp breezes, serene views, and open windows. Sunny days equal happy birds, picnics in parks, carefree jaunts in ponds, forgotten work left for another day. Still, the simple equation remained. This equals that.

So it was with love. He had fought for it for so many years, held it, molded it in his mind, dreamed about it, aggrieved over it, longed for it until the day it was simple: this equals that. This equaled love, not only the love-making, but the equivalency, reciprocity, of having someone, something, on the other side of the equal sign.

The simplicity of the equation, again, hid much deeper meaning. The badge, with its oppressive and all encompassing algorithms, cameras, spies, prisons, cages, couldn't crack the simplest equation of all. Love. Everything fell away when they were together, the angst, anger, frustration, at the oppression, injustice and futility of their efforts at trying to challenge the system. The realisation of what they could accomplish, together, was so much greater. They could create life, love happiness, turn off the lights and disappear for the hours, days, and nothing existed, except them, this equals that.

When they first developed the badge, the creators introduced a controversial new technology called "Predictive Emulator

Technical". This technology justified the expansion of data collection and more reliance on the badge. Once you establish that the technology is valid and serves a purpose then you can identify any limitations not as weaknesses of the technology itself but rather limits on how you use it, work with it, manage it. The technology thus remains unquestioned at its essence and only its inputs, its governance, are doubted. But, when the limitations or weaknesses of those inputs are dictated as results of constraints of the technology itself, the answer is to unleash the algorithms, the equations, the factors so that this equals that equals that equals that equals that, and so on.

The technology doesn't work because it needs data, more numbers, fed into it. Give it more power. No one stops to question why we are giving more power to something that doesn't make sense because to do so would be to acknowledge ignorance. Instead, make this make sense. Advance mankind.

Predictive Emulator Technical or "PET" was an algorithm developed by a brilliant programmer/Yoga instructor whom everyone hailed as a genius. In simple terms, it was able to tell you what you would do before you did it. When fed with the right data, it could sound an alert when the hungry child, eyeing the greasy sandwich, was going to steal. It knew when the child had last eaten; it knew if the child had a propensity for crime either through genetics (there was a criminal gene) or through the child's environment. It could analyse traffic, and depending on the speed, driving conditions, weather, personalities, of the drivers could predict with 9.9999999 accuracy where accidents would occur. It could predict almost anything to a near perfect model. It was mind bogglingly excruciatingly wonderful. Philosophers and moralists, politicians, debated its use, governance, structure. It was too powerful for any one government, or any one any thing to control. Everyone, well nearly everyone, accepted the legitimacy of the PET. The only question was the way it would be used.

The PET also needed more data, vast amounts of data, to work. It needed full access, genetic records, legal systems, weather patterns, histories, and it needed power, extreme amounts of energy.

The PET led to the badge. Government lawyers spent years hashing out how it would be governed and financed.

The algorithm was perfect. In "free" nations, they didn't use PET to arrest preemptively but in others, governments found its power too convenient. The WWSC would cut these nations off but gradually its power made everyone drunk. These "free" nations, drunk on moral authority and rhetoric, routinely got together and used PET to take out "bad guys". Nations lost power. What mattered was who controlled the Badge, and this was by a council led by the Mon, who was voted and approved by nations based proportionally on financial contributions.

Within 20 years, the introduction of this controversial algorithm had changed the course of human history. Because of its predictive power, vast resources were spent on it. It made the world safer. Some diseases disappeared entirely. Violence, murder, rape, within PET countries, dramatically declined. Whether this was because of better nutrition, education, provided to young mothers monitored by the badge, or because the badge required millions of enforcement officers who, armed with authority and power of the badge, found it easier to lock away all "would be" criminals, no one was sure. But crime is bad. No one had an issue with the purse-snatchers being taken off the streets. The noticeable issues began with the artists.

Soon, the PET could predict, based on what you read, what badge pages you visited, what you wrote, what you said, what you would do to a 9.999999 accuracy. If that action was "predictive punishable" as defined by the council, one could find oneself locked away for being curious.

Again, not many complained. Who is against taking away those who would kill innocents to prove a point? But the .0000001 began to add up and soon questions were being asked and trying to dismantle the badge itself became a crime.

For all its complexity, at its heart, the badge was really quite simple: this equals that. The problem was it was wrong. It was wrong because the badge couldn't solve the most simplest, basic yet complex equation of all. It could never, despite all the this equals that equals that equals that equals that equals that, and so on, tell you what a person was thinking.

The human mind was still incomprehensible. Sure, the badge could give you the predictive capacity to the 10th degree but it could never get beside, inside, one's mind, and explore what one was feeling, thinking, wanting. Because it relied on external inputs, people just learned to write and say less. Children were taught to be more careful in school because childhood dalliances would reveal themselves in the badge, ultimately providing a 9.999999 predictive capacity that these former problem children, now adults would make bad employees.

There were several . . . The first was that the changed behavior patterns which rendered the badge useless further emboldened its supporters, and the answer was simply to feed it more data, give it more power, further weakening its ability to serve any real purpose. The second was the creator himself, disappeared, after some cryptic statements about humanity. No one knew where he went but it was suspected he was behind the badge still, hiding, improving it, or hopelessly trying to, while in reality he was doing the opposite. He was hiding in the African forests trying to defeat what he had created.

The irony was that the PET's creator was trying to destroy it and the PET, the greatest predictive algorithm and technology couldn't predict this, or provide a single prediction as to his whereabouts and thoughts.

Yes. It was perfect but it was also useless.

It had changed the world, made it safer, healthier but it removed so much of the meaning behind this equals that. Except that something like a kiss, an embrace over candlelight, all the computers, machines, couldn't replace or interfere with something as simple as young love.

Rico would come home after work, the crowded trains with people on their modules wearing masks, and eagerly walk through the door, removing his mask and understand. The woman with the big eyes from the rich lush land. They could close the blinds, unplug the machines and he was really himself for the first time in his life, no longer constrained by what he could or couldn't say, could or couldn't be. For just a few hours each night, this, her, equaled, that, love.

. . .

Before he left, he remembered his last words, from an ancient text. He complained but the women of the village insisted on anointing him with oil, sweet-smelling, rich, it flowed down his face like blood. Then the ancient text. What were the words?
Our Father. Who Art in Heaven. Hallowed be Thy Name.

Soon, he was in a boat, dropped off in the megapolis' detritus, hustled back to the lobby of the luxury hotel, just in time apparently because there were uniforms there looking concerned. The same lovely idyllic of blue harbour and fashionable young Africans playing on their badge portals was still there. The uniforms were yelling at the small attendant who had earlier in the week pleaded with him not to venture too far. A stern fat man in a suit stood to the side on the phone.

"You're a stupid stupid man. You are a kwasia to let an Oyingbo go off like that. Your Oga go punish you o! Now we must go find this man. You're very stupid!"

The small man was sweating, nervously twisting his shoulders and torso.

"Gentlemen that won't be necessary. I had a river charter to the jungle to see the rare chindesez parrot." The group looked up, silenced by astonishment. Immediately the formerly domineering uniforms were subservient while the attendant showed no sign of reduced anxiety.

"Sir," the uniform who did the talking, the speaking soldier, said, "We are so delighted to see your kind face. It is a miracle that you have returned safe. Sir, there are many wicked people in the bush. The owner of this establishment was very upset."

"Oh don't worry fella," he said slapping the uniform on the back. The speaking soldier flinched and his partner reflectively gripped his rifle tighter, displaying a clear dichotomy between words and thoughts on display.

"Yes sir," the spokesman said, regaining his mild manners. "Sir, we must worry. We had great concerns for our guests in this country." Then the fat man finished his call and approached.

"Ah now we have our adventurous visitor!" The attendant still stood rocking from side-to-side. "Please, come and join me for a tumbler of some excellent scotch?" He looked at the fat man warily. Perhaps sensing his hesitation, he grabbed his shoulder and inched closer. "Let me guess, Harvard? I am a Yale man myself! No love lost between friends eh?"

"No sir. I did not have the privilege. Please, can we have the attendant here arrange a car to the airport as soon as possible." The two soldiers and the fat man reacted with cautious deflation, the attendant; the focus of attention now, appeared to be on the verge of self-defecation.

"Please stay with us Sir. We would like to learn more about your visit to the bush." The speaking soldier said, almost pleading.

"No. No. I want to go now, immediately." The owner and the speaking soldier looked at each other then back at him.

"Okay sir. I will manage one of my contacts now to arrange a flight" the owner said cheerfully and unhelpfully.

"Listen you fat fuck. I just finished trekking three days through this shit hole country to get a picture of a fucking bird."

"Sir, we are all Christians, please . . ."

"No, you listen fat man. Book the damn car now. Not on that phone but have shaky face here pull round the nice little shiny thing parked at the front and drive me immediately or else I will put in a personal call to my embassy about what a shit hole this place is and I mean you personally."

"Well!" the owner replied indignantly.

"Sir there is no need to insult our kindness and our country" the soldier said quietly and earnestly.

"Now" was his reply. The uniforms tensed again. From their expressions, they wanted nothing more than to beat him mercilessly, but the forced smiles remained.

"Akiya, go now! Take my keys!" The fat man barked to the attendant, who managed to go from anxious rocking to a frozen stance. He eventually unfroze after a few seconds and nervously ran to the door, nearly stumbling down the stairs. He wondered whether if he were African like the attendant, whether he would be in prison or on his way to prison right now.

"Thank you sir. You are welcome." The speaking soldier said before he bowed and backed away. He was sure the owner would make a few calls but crucially it wouldn't be an airport request. That kind of message could trigger an algorithm, assign an analyst and within 48 hours, it would be all uncovered. The attendant, now shaking again, didn't have a badge portal. Most people here didn't have full access yet. It was a major policy initiative among the Council that he, the Mon, work to provide this access, to poor countries. He was happy at his lack of any real progress.

At the airport, he gave the attendant all the remaining local currency he had, about two years wages and told him to get a real job, buy a store front and start a discrete guest house for foreigners. His country badly needed it.

. . .

That was two weeks ago. Four additional days of boat rides, ferries, trucks through slim mountain tracks, he arrived back at this supreme position, chairing an emergency situational assessment planning strategy ExCo. The days were difficult. He couldn't wash his mind of the oil or the words of the women, nor the soft water of the river as he sank under.

On Earth. As It Is In Heaven.

Deep in the jungle, these women were gathered around his brother as he delivered what would be his final weekly sermon against the evils of the system he had created and that his brother maintained.

Amazed And Perplexed, They Asked One Another, "What Does This Mean?"
Some, However, Made Fun Of Them And Said, "They Have Had Too Much Wine."

As he was sitting ignoring the monotonous tones of his aides, pretending to be typing into his portal, his mind went back to his brother there, surrounded by believers. The militant ones gathered outside, shooting targets, waiting for the spiritual leader to unleash their anger at his system.

When The People Heard This, They Were Cut To The Heart And Said to Peter And The Other Apostles, "Brother, What Shall We Do?"

"Sir!" one of the aides called out. We have eyes on a counterproductive camp.
"Where?" he asked.
"Looks like . . ." the smartly dressed aide hurriedly typed, "looks like, deep in wooded area, West Africa."

He took a deep breath. He knew. "Tom, please deal with these idiots. I'm going to call the President to inform him." And he got up, went into his closet, and cried.

Peter Replied, "Repent And Be Baptised, Every One of You, In The Name Of Jesus Christ For The Forgiveness Of Your Sins. And You Will Receive The Gift Of The Holy Spirit."

Somewhere in the sky, a glimmer appeared. The soldier man, or Conqueror, slugging away at a tree with a heavy machine gun, caught it in the corner of his eye. It was dusk, and he felt, too early for a bright star.

The Promise Is For You And Your Children And For All Who Are Far Off, For All Whom The Lord Our God Will Call."

A flash. Conqueror remembered everything turning white and awaking bleeding in the bush, body parts cast astern everywhere. The white man was dead.

7.

Passion of a fanatic.

The badge's biggest vulnerability besides the impenetrable nature of the human mind was data security. The algorithm contained and relied on invaluable information that if revealed could create or destroy fortunes, societies, governments, lives.

The algorithm's creator was no data security expert and initially there were several devastating data breaches but then the committee began hiring security experts to develop and refine it. It was one of these early engineers who construed the secure badge that was rumored to be now in charge of the council. It was all rumored. The badge and the council's work was so important and so potentially destructive that its meaning and their activities were state secrets. Everyone within two degrees of power knew who was Mon and who else sat on the council but they only spoke about it in hushed tones at the risk of being labeled subversive and placed on a watch list.

Since these early spates of data leads, there were hardly any additional ones. It never happened or at least was never reported or discussed, so no one thought it occurred. In reality, in addition to the clustered governance structure, there was also a dark underworld to the badge, financed and managed by sophisticated criminals or criminal algorithms.

These programmes took ones badge profile and within milliseconds, propagated trivial purchases in artificial currencies, simultaneously equating them and exploring digital money arbitrage opportunities in the electronic artificial currency exchanges, before depositing into commodity accounts and transacting these into the hard receipts that were still accepted in offline countries for things like minerals and foodstuffs. These receipts entered into the normal flow of commerce in places where there weren't cameras looking down on every hard exchange desk, no powerful algorithms monitoring every transaction. By the time, normally ten or thirty seconds, that it took the badge to halt the transactions and conversions, someone in an offline country had already hit PRINT on millions of criminally falsified receipts.

Most experts warned that this behavior was state-sponsored given its brutal effectiveness and efficiency but they could never deliver the hard evidence against any likely culprits.

All of the fraud was cleverly hidden from the public but in the poor nations that were conduits for the proceeds, it was all too clear in the halls of power. The leaders were all privy (and party) to the fraud. They looked the other way while billions flowed through state coffers. Formerly lowly provincial officials began riding around in the latest most fashionable vehicles and technology.

Additionally the illegal receipts inflated the costs of locally produced commodities such that the poor had a more difficult time purchasing food. And because the ill-gotten gains proved so lucrative, the local leaders had no incentive to stop it. That is, there was no reason to bring the countries online, where greater enforcement would stop the fraud. Their families could travel to the west or to local enclaves where the technology worked. There was no reason to give access to everyone. The underworld, just like the marbled and glassed corridors of the vanguard, had its own unspoken rules, power centres and leaders, and it was just as firmly established.

Rico learned all this from her. He learned that there were covert armies in these poor countries who had learned the technology, and seeing the wholesale destructive characteristics, were committed to changing it. Their strategy was to bring the data leaks to light by exposing the details of millions of citizens in the powerful countries publicly.

The challenge was in the ingenuity of the data fixes implemented decades prior. No single badge portal relied on a single data source. To combat consolidated breaches, each portal relied on data from thousands of different storage machines that could only be understood and confirmed by an algorithm that operated within the badge. Criminal algorithms could combine the portals of one to two profiles at a time but it was challenging to even conceptualise a machine powerful enough to breach the system, obtain access to all the data points, combine these in an algorithm that can translate, and then repeat this for enough profiles to weaken the perception of security, all within a few milliseconds before the security settings shut it down. Such a powerful computer would also have to be capable of hiding or else it would lead back to all those involved, many of whom actually worked for the council.

Despite all this, she thought she had a chance. Watching the fervor in her eyes as she spoke of breaking the system was intoxicating.

Her plan was to use a government machine infiltrated by a rogue programme. She would coordinate a mass password release whereby millions of passwords will be leaked of those who had used machines in public libraries, whose central system she had placed the errant programme. The library would inadvertently leak the info, then three rouge machines would take control of every compromised badge portal but instead of using this to steal an inordinate amount of money, it will publish onto a public website the most intimate details of the lives of those affected, chat logs, lovers photos, business plans. The hope was that such a leak would destroy faith in the badge and create a democratic response in terms of protest and change.

They began working on this plan with the intensity of their love-making. Writing programme equations out by hand over candlelight, he became a convert, taking on an immigrant ethos of belief. Before long, it was his plan. He stopped going into the office, quit his job, instead he spent all this time frenetically writing the code she had taught him, day and night. His hair grew long, his eyes sunk in, possessed by passion, desire and anger. Sometimes, she held his head from behind while he was at the desk, occasionally kissing his overgrown hair, while he sped along, a train racing towards the end, driven manic and ferociously by a calm beautiful conductor.

8.

All the way.

The permanence of the architecture was one reason people hesitated to question the system. The glass and metal facades, domineering yet open, airy, light-filled, reflective even, appeared impossible to dismantle. And they were ubiquitous in every city. An intellectual, well-versed in history could of course imagine that one day society would move on to a different epoch, but even they struggled to conceptualise the process that would precipitate that change or even the resulting theory. The world was already so devastatingly modern and post-modern, who could visualise post-post-modernity? Anyone who claimed they could was dismissed in pleasant company as a mad man, crazed paranoia-infused quack.

But Conqueror knew these buildings could come down. We weren't on the verge or dawn of an era where they would stand for millennia. Instead, we were out of the dawn of an era where everything could radically mutate, shape-shift into new images and concepts.

He used to be a student in Paris when he developed these ideas. He sat on the beaches of the Seine, with his university friends debating the merits of the algorithm, post-modernity, racism, policies, when his views began to diverge. He was tired of debating. He argued that they should forcefully seek to remake society in their image. These were the early days when they started to round up intellectuals who detested the merits of the badge. He was unbowed, giving speeches at the Bastille, openly posting anti-badge messages on counter-websites. His Parisian friends abandoned him. His appearance charged but still no one arrested him.

The buildings must come down became his motto, but alone, wayward, in Paris, he had no outlet, no means of articulating what that meant. Despite the rants, writings, he continued his studies, learning how to programme, discovered that he was gifted. Most of his friends drifted into mediocre employment maintaining websites and communications systems, hiding behind badge portals that mediated their earlier radical views but he refused to conform, or graduate.

How had he arrived here? His father immigrated to an industrial town in northern France from a poor offline country. His father never talked about his home. His mother raised him to be a Frenchman, albeit a poor one from Lille, but he knew he was always different from the way people reacted to his name and his skin color. The anger inside at the system, post-modernity, contemporaneous modes of thinking about the world, the badge, was really anger at his own lack of identity. In a world devoid of meaning, yet full of vacuous glass and metal, his loneliness was peculiarly painful. Bring the buildings down, was his motto.

Listless, idling, he kept protesting and learning the technology, hoping one day to discover a purpose. Unbeknownst to him, his performance on exams kept him out of jail. He was monitored as a prodigy since his early years and assigned an analyst. Many like him developed radical underpinnings early on because they had such a deep understanding of the technology but ultimately when faced with life's complexities that come with age and maturity, wives, husbands, mortgages, parents, jobs, they joined the system.

One day riding a cab back to his student housing from another rally of one, he gave the driver his real name when asked. Spies were everywhere and you never provided a real name if you lacked a badge portal but for some reason he felt comfortable with the driver of this cab. It was a combination of the music, the tone of his voice, his accent. He reminded him of his father. Upon hearing his name, the driver announced that they were members of the same tribe. He then gave him his family history going back centuries. The driver knew what village he hailed from, the accomplishments of his ancestors.

How did he know all that from a name he asked and the driver explained that they hailed from an oral history where badge portals were confined in the minds and on the tongues of succeeding generations. "You can never hide who you are" he said. The driver invited him into his house and he met his wife and children. They had just arrived to France and the food, full of exotic flavour, spices, the music that came from the radio, was unlike anything he had ever experienced. The man had a daughter, quiet, dark, beautiful. She paid attention to him, made sure she was the one who served his food and cleaned his place whenever he came for visits. Her father boastfully talked about her cooking skills. She would blush and hide her face.

He found himself coming several times a week, not for the food, but to see her. He forgot the father and mother were even there. Noticing their engrossing stares at one another, the father allowed them to sit alone in the next room. She remembered everything he told her. She knew his emotions, gave warnings and reassurance to relieve his paranoia. She served him tea and comforting words. He began to discover his identity and meaning, in a woman, in love. He asked her father if he could marry her and was granted permission only if he graduated and found a real job.

Within six months he had found both and in a quiet ceremony at the local magistrates, his father embraced her father and his white French mother wore their tribal native clothes and danced boldly, happily at his wedding.

That night he discovered true love. He had previous relationships, sexual encounters, but the touch of his wife, took him to a new constellation of emotion and serenity. From radical student to lonely technological maintenance operator, he still harbored all the anger and anti-badge views, except now they weren't nearly as important as his wife, who would soon give birth to a daughter.

He also didn't realise he was tagged as a prodigy. At work, he outperformed all the other programmers and bored, he began to write new, more efficient algorithms. His bosses took notice and soon he was promoted. This caused jealously and some colleagues reported him for the controversial political beliefs he still sometimes espoused over lunch. One day, an inspector visited his home while he was at work and spoke to his wife. He went to the police headquarters and slapped the man in the face, all of the anger and rage bubbling up at such a minor indignity. His wife tried to calm him but the icy glances and ostracisation at work unnerved him. He began posting more subversive messages and the increased monitoring that came as a result drove him further to the edge.

He lost his sense of place sometimes, forgot where he was. He would disappear into a haze, wander for days, half-naked, covered in his own feces, until someone called the authorities. Tied down in institutions, it would take a while for them to find his wife who would plead to have him released. She was the only one who could calm him. Spitting, yelling, kicking, while tied to a gurney, only the sound of her voice would bring him peace. Sometimes he would end up in different parts of France altogether, not knowing how a walk from work could result in a mad pain-filled artificially lit room in Marseille, episodes that wouldn't end until he heard a voice, hers, telling him it would all be okay.

Sometimes, months would go between episodes, once even years. He would return to work, but something, some trigger would always send him back. Soon, he was forbidden to leave his home and his wife wasn't allowed to leave him unattended for more than few hours at a time.

Eventually even his wife had a difficult time calming him. His daughter was the only person that now approached him without fear. He played with her over blocks, in the playground behind their large blocks of flats under the watchful eyes of his wife as gently and as caring as any devoted father but at night the shaking and sweating scared his wife and she knew soon even his daughter would be exposed to this side of him. She gave him an ultimatum and began to isolate herself from him, going to her father's for extended periods.

One night, it was the fire and the building came down. He remembered that when she was away the only thing that comforted him were flames. He would awake from his haze watching the gas flames on the stove, wondering how it had started and why he was there. One night he awoke and the entire building was on fire. He heard horrid screams, crying, and sirens. He wasn't sure if his wife and daughter were there, inside, when he opened his eyes laying outside on the cold wet ground under a blanket offered by a firefighter. Next to him were bodies, some children, also covered in blankets and those images sent him running, naked, alone, cold, through the streets of Paris.

He awoke again in a homeless shelter next to long haired hippy who spoke about the destructive nature of the badge. He told the man of a land with hills, rivers, where they could go to destroy it.

The man helped him and in return he helped the man, but the anger still remained. All he kept of his old life was a battered, half burned photo of his beautiful wife and daughter that remained in his hands through the final traumatic episodes. He didn't have any more relapses since but he also didn't know if they lived or died. He cried sometimes, especially at night looking at the photo over a flame away from where the other men could see or hear him. He wanted her touch, her voice, but feared she was already dead and if alive, that he was incapable of doing so as long as the old paranoia, system, anger, technology, remained. She was behind a wall, a fort of glass, steel, buildings, and machines, that he needed to bring down.

9.

Outside the chamber.

That day he emerged from his closet, wiped away his tears and casually submitted his letter of resignation to the President and to the other members of the Council. He was exhausted, he said, the new counterproductives and expansions were taxing his ability to concentrate on the demands of the job.

The reality was that they would find his brother's remains in due course and they would connect the dots. His brother's identity was completely absent from the algorithm but they would be enough information at the site for the forensics analysts to establish it and then once they had obtained his DNA, there was enough information in the algorithm about him to establish that they were brothers.

He always feigned ignorance and anxiety about his brother's disappearance. His ascendancy to the top of the bureaucracy was partly due to the sympathy it engendered among those who knew his background. There were monuments and honorary scholarships erected to honor the architecture his brother had established. His memorial stood as a kind of ideal, model, poor kid who through sheer hard work built and created a technological revolution that saved millions of lives, made the world safer, more green, more interconnected, decreased military conflicts and poverty.

In the echo chamber of hope, media, wealth, modernity, his brother's memory served as the acoustic wall. Outside, the chamber was a completely different reality of pain, repression, sadness, inhibition and isolation that, ironically, claimed his brother as its most prominent victim.

Anytime someone tried to bring glimpses of that reality within the echo chamber there were immediately silenced, sometimes violently. Soon, a forensics team would jump off helicopters, likely in the depths of darkness and scour the fields his brother was toiling in. If anyone survived, they had already or were in the process of fleeing. The agents would take clothes, files, anything they could salvage but more critically they would secure his remains. He wondered in what shape they were in. Was his brother incinerated or did he die from collapsed debris? Would they deliver a small box or an entire casket? Irrespective, once the remains were secured, identical and returned, the truth would be known and he would reside outside the echo chamber, forever, and so would his brother's memory. The system had to continue. He knew that, but how. In what form, was no longer any of his concern, because he was no longer part of it.

The President accepted his resignation letter, he said, with great shock and remorse, but presidents always enjoyed the patronage and control that came with a new Mon. Radcliffe appeared shocked when he walked into his office. The Mon never went to that floor. He got on the elevator and walked through the halls. Startled staff walked past him nervously. He went into Radcliffe's office suite and his front assistant tried to both type an alert into the key pad and be cordial and respectful to the visiting Mon. She did a horrible job, mumbling "why hello, hello, um, hello Mr. Mon" while trying to type something clumsingly into the keypad.

"Oh don't worry, Ann, is it? Trust me. He is not going to be upset after he hears what I'm going to say."

He never beat around the bush in anything he did. He was reminded of the change in power dynamic between now and then, when Radcliffe, shaking hands, received the news that he was resigning. He appeared at the time conflicted between jubilation and eagerness to position himself for the promotion and express faux sadness at the loss of a colleague. At that time he looked at Radcliffe's face and felt sick, both at the raw ambition on display and at what the badge and the system had become. "Radcliffe, don't worry. You can count on my support as the next Mon. You're going to come out of this good." He noticeably relaxed, not as conflicted and a little less guarded. "Thank you Mr. Mon but what about you? What will you do? How are you?" He remembered his tone then and wondering whether there was actually a touch of sincerity behind the questions. There were no doubts about that now, as Radcliffe sat in his living room bearing a small box, his face, tone and words conveying a clear message of passive and quiet hostility. A few weeks before he was a lonely AsMon who had been maneuvering for Mon his entire career of thirty odd years. Many like him had been passed over, remaining forever in the muck of obscurity, but now he was cloaked in the full spectrum of presidential authority, confident, polished, leonine in the Mon's uniform.

"Cliff, we have a problem" he said nodding towards the small box between them. "I think you know what's in that box." They had come at dawn, storming down his quiet suburban street in a large convoy. He always preferred a single car with a driver and a guard, whom he viewed naively as a required annoyance but this Mon obviously viewed the job differently. He doubted his neighbors knew that he did any thing important or official until today. They cordoned off the entire street with beefy shaded suits standing outside his front door. Inside, sitting around his living room coffee table, was just he and the shiny Mon.

"For Christ's sake Radcliffe, did you have to bring the entire Third Infantry to have a chat at 6 am on a Sunday morning? You're going to freak out my neighbors." Radcliffe seemed a little surprised and taken aback, confused that anyone would question the Mon's entourage.

"Cliff, listen, I'm the Mon now. That's Mr. Mon" he asserted seeking to regain a semblance of control. "It's unfortunate but, we're at war and security is critical." He signed and threw his hands up. He was dressed in a bathrobe and his hair was still wet from a recently completed shower. He grabbed his cup of coffee and stood up, his back to the Mon, who remained seated, unfazed, in front of the small box.

"War. War. War. The way you people talk it's as if war was one of those video games, as if it were a feeling, a mood, an oeuvre."

"You people? This is a war you started need I remind you."

"War I started, this is a war you started" he repeated in a mocking tone. "You've already sucked into this stupid political blame game posturing bullshit. Yes I know I started it and you intend to finish it, blah blah, save the sound bite bullshit for someone who cares."

"I beg your pardon Cliff. I didn't come here to argue. I know this is difficult. I only came here to, to-"

"You came here to bring me the remains of my older brother," he said sitting back down. He placed his hands on his face after sitting the coffee down. He wanted to cry. He knew he would cry if he looked at the box but he couldn't cry now. He pulled his hands through his hair and sighed again, deeply.

"Cliff listen, as I said, I know this is difficult. We know everything. We know about the little trip you took. That's enough to imprison you for counterproductive collaboration."

"Yes, of course you do. Now arrest me," he said putting his hands out in a handcuff gesture. He thought he could discern a slight smirk underneath the outwardly dour expression of the shiny new Mon. He had firmly established his control.

"Now Cliff, no one wants to do that. Your family has given a lot to this country. Your brother was a great hero for what he established and help build." So that was their angle, secret it away, hide it. That was disappointing he thought. Such a secret would eventually become public with devastating consequences, but now he understood the real purpose of the visit.

"Okay Mr. Mon, thank you so much for visiting. As you can imagine, when my brother contacted me, I didn't know what to do. I decided to go see him before making any decisions to try and talk some sense into him. I hadn't seen or heard for him for over twenty years."

"Yes, we know. Listen Cliff the President is on your side here."

"Thank god Mr. Mon. As you know, upon my return, while still dealing with my brother's new path, I never interfered with any investigation. In fact, I probably authorised the," his voice wobbled with emotion, "I probably authorised the strike that killed him."

"Yes, that's why no one is blaming you here. The President is still deciding on a course of action but so far it's all positive for you, well as positive as it can be, under the circumstances," he said, nodding at the box.

"Thank you Mr. Mon." The shiny new Mon got up to leave, walking out his front door, he turned and said "Oh and Cliff, the President thinks you should stay put for a while. These security guys will stick around if that's okay. I'll tell them to stay in the car a little down the street. You can go do little errands and stuff in the area but don't venture too far."

"Yes Mr. Mon, understood. That's perfectly fine."

Later that night, the shiny new Mon would tell the President that the old tarnished director seemed shaken but was willing to "play ball".

He watched him leave, ever more disgusted. He thought back on his brother's words.

I am at peace right here, right now, because you are with me.

He held the box that night, sobbing, screaming inwardly, sadness, despair, forever outside the chamber.

10.

The beast.

Though the metaphor has been made many times by many writers to describe systems and paradigms like the badge, the octopus remains as close to perfect as any living organism can be.

It never ceases to become more intelligent in old age, as it ages, the older, the larger, the stronger, the more perfect it is. This is because its brain is amorphous; it doesn't stem from a single mass. There is no central locus, trust or focus but its entire organism is its brain and as it gets older, bigger, so do the millions of synapses and electrons and neurons that flow through its fluid connections. Its eyes are often the largest solid mass it has, which gives it the ability to contort, shrink, squeeze within any space that it can fit its eyes through.

It has no childhood to speak of. Often it floats as an inseminated embryo, a sort of pseudo-plankton, on the surface of oceans, in danger at any time of being swallowed by a whale, or one of the other myriad plankton-eaters, for months, before suddenly sinking to the bottom and exploding in size. Within a year, it has grown infinitesimally and it never stops growing until it dies.

Highly adaptive, it can survive in and out of water. It can swim, motor on land, tunnel underground. It has unparalleled eyesight for the natural world, with the ability to see sharply in nearly any kind of light condition. The octopus can also change colour, nearly disappearing into a background of rocks and sand. Like so many living things, its only major weakness is the irresistible urge to reproduce, which kills, ultimately, both mother and father, never to see, know or influence their millions of offspring, lucky enough to survive that float to the surface before sinking to the ground. This creature is simply remarkable.

Nonetheless, all these things are not why writers, artists and philosophers so often equate the octopus with evil. Although, any of these traits, invisibility, amorphous intelligence, monster-like growth, nonexistent familial bonds or values, or its non-familial and self-destructive sexual nature, could very easily provide any artist with enough palettes to paint a vivid portrait of evil. No. It is the undulating, gripping and interwoven nature of the octopus' tentacles that capture our imagination. We observe in awe a creature that can seemingly grab, taste, devour, and destroy everything within its reach. Lust, greed, gluttony, all-consuming power, the octopus is typically analogous for all these things as they relate to man's existence, in the artist's eye.

Thus, the octopus was evil and so was the badge. The sign of the octopus became a silent protest. One-by-one, people began to replace their smiley computer-generated images with those of the almighty octopus. Something was happening; a protest, revolt was growing.

There was no focal point, no centre. Different movements were planning apocalyptic action in tandem, as if connected through millions of undetected connections flowing through malleable veins. A conversation, a picture, a poem, a song, a knowing look, embrace, all coming from the only solid mass within the entire system, the badge.

All organisms become unsustainable if there are no limits, no moderation, reticence or austerity. A multitude of power centres is a fantastical asset until it becomes a multitude of unrest, or a multitude of determined self-destruction. The eyes see but there are no longer in control. They follow where the army, and ever-growing brain stretched throughout the thickening tentacles, lead. And ultimately, as we all know, the seemingly invincible beast dies.

www.ingramcontent.com/pod-product-compliance
Lightning Source LLC
Chambersburg PA
CBHW060047150626
46556CB00018BA/3107